Wait for Me!

An Ivy and Mack story

T0337045

Written by Juliet Clare Bell
Illustrated by Gustavo Mazali

Collins

Who and what is in this story?

Listen and say

Mum

Ivy

Mack

Croc

Dad

beach

Mack says, "I love the beach!"
Ivy says, "Me too!"

Mack says, "I love the sand and I love the sea!"

Ivy says, "Look! ICE CREAM!"

Ivy says, "OK! But I would like an ice cream! And to go in the sea!"

Croc and I are getting some water.

7

Mum says, "Let's have an ice cream *after* we finish the sandcastle."

Mum says, "... and after I finish my book!"
Dad says, "Get more water, Ivy."

Dad says, "It's big."
Mack says, "*VERY* big."

10

Ivy says, "The sea is beautiful!"

Mack! Dad!
Where are you?

Ivy says, "Mack! Dad! Are you getting an ice cream?"

Mack says, "Ivy! Ivy! There you are!"

Dad says, "Ivy, are you OK?"

Ivy says, "Yes, here I am. I'm OK."

Ivy says, "Now we're here, let's have an ice cream!"

Dad says, "Yes, let's have an ice cream. And let's get Mum an ice cream, too."

Mack says, "Mum likes chocolate ice cream! Me too."

Mack says, "Wow! I love
our sandcastle."

Ivy says, "Let's go in the sea now!"

Mack says, "We *ARE* in the sea now.
Look!"

Picture dictionary

Listen and repeat

beach

ice cream

sand

sandcastle

sea

1 Look and order the story

2 Listen and say

Collins

Published by Collins
An imprint of HarperCollins*Publishers*
Westerhill Road
Bishopbriggs
Glasgow
G64 2QT

HarperCollins*Publishers*
1st Floor, Watermarque Building
Ringsend Road
Dublin 4
Ireland

William Collins' dream of knowledge for all began with the publication of his first book in 1819.

A self-educated mill worker, he not only enriched millions of lives, but also founded a flourishing publishing house. Today, staying true to this spirit, Collins books are packed with inspiration, innovation and practical expertise. They place you at the centre of a world of possibility and give you exactly what you need to explore it.

© HarperCollins*Publishers* Limited 2020

10 9 8 7 6 5 4 3 2

ISBN 978-0-00-839729-6

Collins® and COBUILD® are registered trademarks of HarperCollins*Publishers* Limited

www.collins.co.uk/elt

British Library Cataloguing in Publication Data

A catalogue record for this publication is available from the British Library.

Author: Juliet Clare Bell
Illustrator: Gustavo Mazali (Beehive)
Series editor: Rebecca Adlard
Publishing manager: Lisa Todd
Product managers: Jennifer Hall and Caroline Green
In-house editor: Alma Puts Keren
Project manager: Emily Hooton
Editor: Deborah Friedland
Proofreaders: Natalie Murray and Michael Lamb
Cover designer: Kevin Robbins
Typesetter: 2Hoots Publishing Services Ltd
Audio produced by id audio, London
Reading guide author: Julie Penn
Production controller: Rachel Weaver
Printed and bound by: GPS Group, Slovenia

MIX
Paper from
responsible sources

FSC
www.fsc.org

FSC™ C007454

This book is produced from independently certified FSC™ paper to ensure responsible forest management.

For more information visit: **www.harpercollins.co.uk/green**

Download the audio for this book and a reading guide
for parents and teachers at www.collins.co.uk/839729